The Moon Crystal

Dr Adyasha Acharya

Ukiyoto Publishing

All global publishing rights are held by

Ukiyoto Publishing

Published in 2024

Content Copyright © Dr Adyasha Acharya
ISBN 9789367952047

All rights reserved.
No part of this publication may be reproduced,
transmitted, or stored in a retrieval system, in any form
by any means, electronic, mechanical, photocopying,
recording or otherwise, without the prior permission of
the publisher.

The moral rights of the authors have been asserted.

This is a work of fiction. Names, characters, businesses,
places, events, locales, and incidents are either the
products of the author's imagination or used in a fictitious
manner. Any resemblance to actual persons, living or
dead, or actual events is purely coincidental.

This book is sold subject to the condition that it shall not by
way of trade or otherwise, be lent, resold, hired out or
otherwise circulated, without the publisher's prior
consent, in any form of binding or cover other than that in
which it is published.

www.ukiyoto.com

This book is dedicated to my family, friends and readers.

The Moon Crystal

If you think that having your family member in a lead position will have its perks, then you are wrong. So damn wrong.

My grandmother is the leader of the Shadowmoon Coven of witches and warlocks and apparently, she can't just live peacefully without giving me work.

I just arrived today morning after visiting the new alpha of the werewolf pack of this region to negotiate terms with him. Both old and new. And now my grandmother wants to see me in her study.

"What is all this about?" I ask my best friend Irene taking in the sites of the disturbed and gloomy faces of the witches and warlocks.

Our coven is a hybrid one. We don't just have witches. We have warlocks too. These are modern times after all. And we don't have any strong rules except for that everyone here should be loyal.

"Better that you hear it from your parents or your grandmother."

That's suspicious. What kind of thing it is that my best friend can't share it with me? It has to be something important.

"Dad," I wave at my father who is waiting outside my grandmother's study with a worried look on his face. I don't see Mom anywhere though.

Dad gives me a faint smile. "Morning, honey." His light brown hair rests on his shoulder. I get everything from my mother. The dark brunette hair and onyx eyes. But I have added pink highlights to the terminal strands.

"Where is Mom?"

"Making a list of supplies that the novices will be collecting today."

The new witches and warlocks are trained by Mom and a few others. They are taught to use their magic, use weapons, how to cast spells, make potions.

Right now, Mom is making a list of supplies that we use in our potions, especially the healing poultices. That is what the novices shall be collecting from the woods today.

"And why is everyone in a hustle here?" It is as if people are preparing for a war. Our coven isn't the violent type. We don't fight other supernaturals unless and until, they start it. They haven't, have they now?

I talked to the new alpha yesterday. He seemed cool. It isn't like he would have behaved nicely with me and then called a war on us. And we only have a few vampires in this region. The fae, they tend to stay invisible. And there is no other coven around here. So I can conclude there is no war going to happen.

Then why is everyone on the edge?

"Stop whispering in the hallway and come inside, you two," my grandmother shouts from inside.

Irene shrugs. "I'll be in the living room."

Each member of our coven lives here in this mansion, which is inside the property owned by us, the Karlingtons.

Dad steps inside first to face the wrath of his mother. "Mother, I think we should let Althea stay out of this."

"Stay out?" Dorothea Karlington hisses. "She is one of our highly skilled witches. And she is very good at communicating with other supernaturals."

"I am still standing here," I mumble rolling my eyes.

"You shouldn't interrupt when two elders are chatting," Grandma states coldly.

"You called me here. Like literally."

If she doesn't have anything important to say, I should leave. I don't know what happened in just two days that I left this place. I should ask Mom.

"The Moon crystal has been stolen," Grandma confesses before I can leave.

"You didn't just say what I think you did." The Moon crystal can't just be stolen. It was heavily protected.

Dad nods grimly. "Mom is right. The Moon crystal was stolen yesterday night. The two warlocks guarding it were heavily injured and one witch who tried to stop the intruder nearly died."

What the hell? "And why am I being told about this now?"

"You were on your way back here so we didn't want you to worry about it."

"Dad, seriously."

"It doesn't matter anymore. You know the truth now," Grandma says like it is not a big deal that I didn't know about this earlier.

As if hiding it from me for whole three hours and then revealing it to me won't make me angry. Well, ignoring my feelings for this once, I focus on the current situation.

"How the hell did he even get past our wards?" I ask confused. Our protection spell is strong enough to keep anyone out.

"There is only one warlock strong enough to do that- Castor."

Oh, hell!

Castor is a warlock who practices dark magic. He had been in prison for over a decade for injuring few other witches and warlocks while casting a spell.

He was released recently after his sentence was over. And now he deserves to be in the prison again.

"Our coven members will live, right?"

"They will," Grandma replies. "But we need to find the Moon crystal."

"Right."

The Moon crystal is a powerful relic containing huge amount of magic. It has been under our protection for decades. And someone stealing it from under our nose makes it a thousand times worse.

"Okay, so how are we going to find him?"

Grandma looks at me for a moment. "You will."

"What?" I blurt shocked. It is one thing to send me as an ambassador but searching a dark warlock is beyond my experience.

"You can find him. You have a lot of connections."

"That is just expecting too much from me. You don't obviously expect me to do this alone."

Dad turns to Grandma. "Tell her that too?"

"Tell me what?"

"We have requested a warlock from the supernatural prison where Castor was being kept to assist you in finding me."

Great, she has done that even. Only left the hardest thing for me to do. With someone I don't even know. Ugh, I hate this.

"Who is the person?" I inquire curiously.

"He will be here soon and then you can discuss how to find Castor."

Absolutely great. I turn on my heels and stomp out of the room. Outside, I see my cousin Bree and her parents working on the wards. Shimmering blue light shines from their hands as they restore the protection wards around our property.

I leave them to it and make way to the swing in our lawn. Taking a deep breath, I sit down and let the fresh air surround me.

At times like this, it is really hard for me to control my emotions. And when witches and warlocks can't control their emotions, chaos happens.

Footsteps approach me and I swear to God I am going to slap anyone who comes and bothers me right now.

"What-" I angrily stand up and meet a pair of the bluest ever eyes.

"Whoa, that's some temper," a rich voice remarks. The ocean blue eyed stranger has dark raven hair which rests on his forehead. He is wearing a leather jacket over a grey t-shirt and dark jeans.

I know he is lethal just from his presence. This warlock is too powerful.

"Sorry, I just. Nevermind."

He chuckles. "I didn't mind but I appreciate you apologizing for such a small thing."

Is he charming like that or just trying to make a conversation? "Hi," I say finally getting a good glance at the handsome face. Oh my God! This is Shane Windsor. The son of the Warlock in charge of the prison.

"Hey. It is good to see you."

"Yup, you too." We had met when I had been sent to transfer a witch who had gone crazy after power. It was three months ago. But I had liked Shane on the very first meeting.

He is funny, kind and powerful. Like the perfect guy. But he is lethal. His magic can burn a warlock into ashes.

And the guy spends his whole time in the prison. His work is his life. "Thanks for coming here to help me with this."

"I had to come. This is a serious issue." He glances around at my coven members. "Can we go talk somewhere private?"

"Sure."

What secret Shane has to share with me now? I am not that angry with Grandma anymore. At least not about the part where she arranged a stranger to assist me with this case.

Shane isn't a stranger. I had spent one day with him but that is better than someone whom I never knew at all. We also kept in touch through texts. But him being here in front of me is different.

"I am glad it is you handling this case," he says with a grin. He looks like he has jumped out from a fantasy romance novel cover.

"My grandmother will be really happy to hear that. Can you say it again so that I can record it for her?"

He spreads his hands. "Sure."

I laugh. "That was a joke."

"I was damn serious." We both laugh together. "But, honestly didn't you want to take up this case?"

"Honestly, I didn't get a choice exactly. So I was kind of pissed." I don't know why I confessed in front of Shane but I was really frustrated and had to tell someone.

"And here I thought you would be happy to see me. That is the only reason why I took this case. I get to see you again."

That was direct. I blush. "Really?"

"Yes. Aren't you happy to see me?" he raises a brow.

"Haha, yes definitely, I am." I didn't think I would see him here.

"Before we get to work, I want you to promise me that after we have put Castor behind the bars, you are going on a date with me. I wanted to ask you out a lot of times but thought if it would have been wrong in a text message."

I stare at him speechless. Wow. I guess I am not on this road alone. "Okay. Deal."

"I'll hold you to that, Al."

I take Shane to my chamber in the first floor where I do the desk jobs. I don't usually do the desk jobs because I am always away on some mission.

"What did you want to talk about?"

"I wasn't in favour of letting Castor out of the prison. However, the elder members decided that he had completed his term and keeping someone beyond their sentence was unethical. It would have questioned our system."

I agree with Shane but can't also say that the elders were wrong. Every prisoner is let out the day their sentence ends. We couldn't just keep one only because we know he can cause trouble.

Though he did and we are here.

"I guess we'll just have to ignore that and focus on capturing him."

He sighs threading his fingers through his hair. "You are right."

"So, where do we start?"

He clicks his fingers and few papers appear over my desk. Warlocks show off so much. "These are the list of all his acquaintances he used to work with before being welcomed into the prison."

I smile at his usage of words. "This is a really long list," I say scanning the twenty names.

"I know it is pointless. But Dad told I should take it with me. Anyways." He crumples that piece of paper and throws it in the trash can. That was real quick.

"I bet you brought something else too."

He smirks. "Of course, darling. Here look at this." He shows me a picture on his phone. "These are the properties owned by Castor. We didn't confiscate them because his imprisonment was for two decades not lifelong."

I take a look at the properties. One is here on our island. He has six other properties, one each in India, Los Angeles, Russia, Italy, Ireland and Australia.

It will take us a lot of time to find him if we go through each of his properties one by one. By the time we go to the right place, he would be gone eventually.

"Okay. If he has taken the crystal, he must have taken it to unlock the magic in it. For that he will require some time and security. Which of these properties of his is the least accessible?"

"My answer would be the one in Ireland. Because the rest others are in populous and popular cities. That is the only one in located in an isolated place."

"Where exactly?"

"In Greenrocks Island. Never been there."

Me neither. I have heard about it though. "It is a ghosted island. Dad had once gone there years ago."

"We could check it out first."

"Yeah, I'll ask Dad to transport us there."

I leave Shane in my chamber and head to the infirmary where Dad would be. His healing magic is the best so he would be helping our coven members to heal.

The injured members lie, covered in bandages and poultices while Dad works his magic.

"Dad," I wave at him from the threshold. I don't want to disturb the resting witch and warlocks so I stay out of the room.

Dad approaches me. "I saw Shane Windsor talking to you. Have you two discussed the case yet?"

"Yes, we have and I think you guys should hear it out."

Dad, Mom, Grandma, Shane and I gather in the conference hall to discuss our plan. Grandma doesn't seem convinced really but listens to whatever we say patiently.

"He is a warlock, Grandma," I remind her, the fact. "He could be anywhere in the world, truly speaking."

"Althea is right," Shane supports me. "There is like a one in a million chance that we would find him if we try the conventional way."

"There are other ways to find him actually," Grandma points out.

"Yes, like tracking him down. But we don't exactly have something that belongs to him," I protest. This conversation is only delaying us from finding Castor.

Grandma glances at me. "I am sure we can arrange something."

"But we still can't track him because he isn't foolish enough to let us do that. I am sure he has cast a spell to block us from tracking him down."

Dad puts a hand on Grandma's shoulder. "You have given them the job, Mom. Let them do it their way."

"They are efficient enough to do it," Mom says encouragingly.

Shane and I glance at each other as Grandma agrees. "Dad, I need you to create a portal for us to the Greenrocks Island."

"Sure, dear. However, it will take some time."

Witches use blood magic so our ways are different. Warlocks use their earthly connection to cast spells.

It takes Dad roughly ten minutes to create the portal. "Be careful, children," Mom says before we step through the portal.

Night has fallen in the island already. And the portal has landed us in a broken down stone building.

I conjure up a light ball in my hand to illuminate the place.

"What a great place to do something stupid," Shane mutters from behind me.

I stop walking and he slams into me. "Sorry for that. I was wondering how to search for him now."

"Yeah, well…"

"We could trace dark magic," I suggest.

"Yeah, let us do it fast then."

Shane illuminates the place with small sparks of light and I quickly draw back my light ball. He crosses his arms and stands guard. Shadows dance across his face from the light rays.

I sit down on a stone and close my eyes. I have to concentrate to get it done fast.

"You know, tracing dark magic is risky," he whispers softly. His voice is low but it is the loudest thing I can hear right now.

"I know."

"It can draw you in. Be careful."

I nod and take a deep breath. Tracing dark magic is dangerous. I have seen witches and warlocks try it and get crazy. They lose their minds permanently.

I reach out for the tendrils of dark magic near us. I just hope and wish Castor is here and that he hasn't unlocked the magic of the crystal yet.

Dark waves of smoke fill my mind. He is here somewhere. "Althea, did you find him?" Shane's voice is far away now.

"Yes, he is here but I have to find out where exactly."

"Don't pull in too deep."

"I won't." Shane says something but I barely register it. My mind is covered with dark clouds and smoke.

Darkness tries to engulf me and I fight it back. The connection breaks abruptly and I sway forward. Shane catches me in time to stop me from falling. "I got you."

"I am impresses," a new voice laughs. "You did find me." Castor approaches us slowly, his face covered with dark hood. "Your magic was so strong that it forced me to come to you."

Inside his cloak lies the Moon crystal. Its magic is so strong that it calls me towards it.

"Return the crystal," Shane snarls at him. The lethal warlock that was hiding beneath that charm is out in the open now.

"Absolutely not." Castor conjures up fireballs and sends them flying in our direction.

Shane creates a shield to protect us. I trust Shane's magic but Castor is strong and he is pulling some of his energy from the crystal.

"You need to distract him," I whisper to Shane.

"What are you going to do? Don't get too close to him, Al."

"That is the only way I can retrieve that crystal."

"It is too risky."

"We don't have another choice." I create a veil around us. If risky it is, then I am going to take one more tonight. I stand up on my tiptoes and press my lips to his. Shane grabs my waist with his free hand and pulls me closer.

"I am not finished," he says then lets me go. "We'll continue this later."

I pull the veil down and conjure up a blade. Shane dissolves the shield and throws energy balls in Castor's direction. He dodges. I use my blade to hit him. Castor manages to save the crystal from falling though.

Shane summons two fire blades and sends it in Castor's direction. I create a shield over me and they hit Castor in the shoulder.

The crystal drops from his hand and I quickly grab it.

Castor grunts in frustration and uses dark magic to target us. Well, if he can use the crystal's magic so can I. I glance at Shane. "Together?"

"Together, darling."

Both Shane and I summon our whole energy and I use the crystal's magic to amplify it. We send it in Castor's direction. It hits the warlock and his body crumbles into dust. I guess Castor won't be returning to the prison but the crystal will be returning home.

Shane turns to me, grinning. "So, what do you think? Where shall we go on our first date?"

About the Author

Dr Adyasha Acharya

Dr Adyasha Acharya, a doctor by profession, residing in India is a bibliophile. She has written several books including The Fearless Warriors, The Guardian Trilogy, The Crown Heist and has published various short stories and pocket books.

www.ingramcontent.com/pod-product-compliance
Lightning Source LLC
LaVergne TN
LVHW041603070526
838199LV00047B/2121